Office HOURS

AbraXus Tasker College
Freshman Year

Office
Hours

Ali Whippe

4 Horsemen
Publications, Inc.

4 Horsemen
Publications, Inc.

4 Horsemen Publications, Inc.
1497 Main St. Suite 169
Dunedin, FL 34698
4horsemenpublications.com
info@4horsemenpublications.com

Cover & Typesetting by Battle Goddess Productions

Ebook ISBN: 978-1-64450-025-5

Paperback ISBN: 978-1-64450-092-7

Audiobook ISBN: 978-1-64450-026-2

DEDICATION

To J, for the naughty dream

TABLE OF CONTENTS

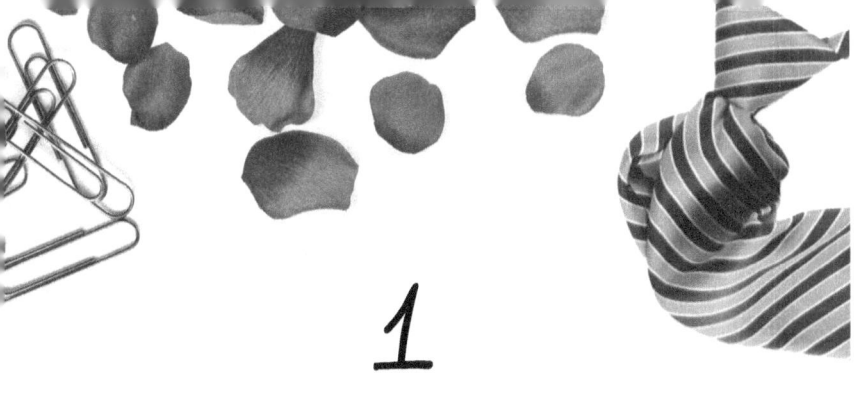

1

The professor isn't in the habit of picking up strange men and bringing them home, but she's always willing to learn something new. A one-night stand is an experience she always wanted to have, and tonight seems like the perfect time. And he is perfect: dark hair just long enough to wind her fingers in, eyes with a hint of mischief, a mouth that looks like it was made for trouble. A body strong enough to lift her up when things get heated combined with long, delicate fingers that promise to find all the right places. Her skin shivers just from meeting his eyes across the room.

The stranger is dressed in a simple blue button down shirt, top button opened at the collar to let him breathe, and loose khakis, his lanky form lounging casually against the wall near the bar. He nurses a drink, liquid amber in a small tumbler, remnants of melting ice cubes clinking along the bottom. He gestures at her with the glass when she meets his eyes, a look of pure invitation, desire in his dark eyes. She makes her way over to him slowly, careful of each step, not trying too hard to be sexy, focusing so that she doesn't trip and make a fool of herself. She's had a few drinks and it is starting to show.

The professor isn't particularly alluring. She isn't bad, of course, but a solid six out of ten. Her breasts are large, her ass is round, and her legs both work fine. Her face is acceptable, but she'll never see it looking back at her from a magazine. In the past, most of her relationships have been based on her brain. She's smart, clever, and sometimes funny. She's a fun-to-be-around, easy going, casual flirt. She doesn't wear high heels or short skirts. She rarely wears makeup at all, though tonight she has splurged on some eyeliner—not that it is particularly visible behind her glasses. Her hair is short and simply cut, her body a little softer than it should be, but still perfectly functional. The few men she's had relationships with haven't complained, but they haven't written any sonnets praising the virtues of her form either.

She usually sticks with the chatting, a little flirting, some innuendos. She never pursues things after that. It always seems like too much effort. If she meets someone she wants to date, she'll want to get to know him first, talk with him and see who he is.

Not this time.

She doesn't particularly want to date the stranger near the bar.

She doesn't care about his childhood winters spent ice skating on the pond. She doesn't care about the novel he is inevitably going to write someday. She doesn't care about his car, or his condo, or his clothes.

Well, maybe his clothes.

Okay, she cares a lot about his clothes. That shirt and its buttons, those little plastic circles practically begging her to release them, pop them free one by one as she runs her hands down his chest. Would he be hairy? She takes another look, scanning those hands again, eyes ranging up his wrists. Maybe.

Her gaze finds his face again, and he is still watching her as she watches him. Her expression must tell him everything he wants to know. She's never had much of a poker face.

Steeling herself, she takes the last few steps toward him, her eyes boldly meeting his. She wants to say something sexy, something clever, but the words die in her throat. How does one normally begin? Introductions, of course. He will ask her name. She will reply and ask his.

But she doesn't want to know his name. She doesn't want to know anything except how it will feel to have those hands pressed against the small of her back, those lips hard against her own, her fingers twined in that dark mop of hair. She wonders if he will take his glasses off to fuck. He seems the type. She always keeps hers on. She's blind without them, and she likes to see what's going on.

They stare at each other, and she waits for him to speak. He doesn't. He just keeps looking at her, the same smolder kept just under wraps. She decides that she has to have him.

"Come with me." She had meant to ask it, to phrase it as a question, but it comes out as a command, and she lets it.

He nods and places the glass in his hand on an empty table. He takes her hand and lets her lead him through the warm bodies in the bar, hands a slow tentative connection of skin as they make their way around the other people. She likes how his fingers alternately press against her palm and twine between her fingers, sensitive skin responding to the different pressures.

She tries to think of where to bring him. The back room doesn't seem likely. She doesn't know this place well enough to know of a secret hidden room somewhere. The restroom will be filled with people, so that is out. She also isn't quite lost to lust enough to consider fucking in a dingy stall. Not tonight anyway. She has some standards, and comfort is one of them. Cleanliness is up there too. She sees the sign pointing to the restroom and turns the other direction, tugging him down a long hallway that leads to an exit door. Outside is a good start.

As they break through the door into the humid night air and hear it slam behind them, she turns back to face him, linked hands tugging him closer. He doesn't hesitate, pulling her into him for a kiss that is all promise of good things to come. She lets herself melt into him, revelling in the feel of his lips on hers, the warmth of his breath on her tongue. His hand presses against her face, holding her to him, and her fingers find their way into that hair, using it to pull him even closer. He groans as she tugs, and their feet stumble a bit, and then he is pressing her against the wall of the building, cold concrete blocks spreading a chill through her back.

He is strong, one arm reaching around to lift her up, hand firmly gripping the curve of her ass as they kiss, her legs wrapping themselves around his hips, excited to feel the hardness pressing against her. His mouth grows more insistent, and she is glad that she is wearing a skirt. His hand leaves her face and reaches down between her legs, fingers rubbing exactly where she wants them. He pushes aside the edge of her panties, and she shudders as his skin touched hers. She moans against his mouth, sucking on his upper lip as his fingers grow more insistent.

"Yes," she moans, pressing herself against him, needing that rhythm to continue, feeling the slow satisfying burn begin low in her belly. "God yes."

She shudders her release against his hand, his fingers pausing to let the moment shatter her, and she sags against him, lips still pressed against his. She feels him smile, and he kisses her again, tentative at first, wondering if she is done or wants more.

She is not done.

She opens her eyes and gives him a slow languid smile as her hands work their way to his belt. He lets her down slowly, letting her feet take the weight carefully as her legs wobble just a little. She unbuckles his belt with steady hands and bated breath, fingers quickly unbuttoning his pants and reaching within. She knows from the bulge pressing against her while they kissed that she will not be disappointed, but it is still a relief to find a sizable cock inside. She pushes him through the hole in his boxers so his pants won't fall down while they stand there, sure to caress every inch of him as she does so. He inhales sharply as she grips his shaft, hooded eyes watching her intently. His hands wander back to her hips, a question in his cocked eyebrow as he lifts her slowly, pulling her toward him as they lean against the wall. He presses the tip of his cock against her, and she pushes back against him, aching to feel the length inside of her, their skin separated by the thin fabric of her panties.

"Please," she moans against his lips as he presses closer into her, and then she is reaching down between them, fingers pushing her panties aside to allow him access. He bites her lip as he enters her, hands splaying beneath her ass as he presses himself inside. She kisses him hard as he pulls back, and then thrusts into her again. She uses the motion to push herself off the ground, rocking her hips back and wrapping her legs around his hips. His hands slide around to her sides, one running down to grip her thigh where it wraps around his hip, the other slipping up to grip her chin and hold her face close as they kiss, his hips pumping rhythmically against her, his cock stroking every inch of her, building and pulsing until she cries out against his lips, and he holds her steady as she shudders.

"Look at me," he orders, voice rough, and she opens her eyes to see him watching her as she comes on his cock, his face a study in desire. "Again," he demands, "Come again," and then he is fucking her again, harder and harder against the wall, and that pulsing brilliance is back in her belly, and she knows she is going to do as he commands.

"Yes!" she yells, but the word is lost in his mouth as he kisses her again, and she loses herself again to the rhythm, to the blinding need that drove her to go out in the first place. Finally, she thinks, finally! Good-God-fucking yes-finally! And then he is slowing down, waiting for her to come back to herself, and they meet one another there, in that perfect place of satisfaction, where it's enough, definitely enough, but there's also the chance for one more, just one more moment of ecstasy. He reads her mind, or her face, or her body, and kisses her again, slowly this time, letting the moment build as it will, their bodies entwined against the wall, all thoughts of anything else but one another forgotten. There is just his mouth, and her hands in his hair, and his hands on her warm skin, and his cock hard and throbbing inside her sliding sweetly back and forth, back and forth, and when she can't stand it anymore, she tugs his hair and makes him look at her. "Now," she commands him. "Come for me. Now."

His rhythm doesn't change, doesn't increase, but keeps on in a steady pulse, and she lets the orgasm shatter her as it does him, bodies shuddering together, and then they are slowly sliding down the wall, her ass landing in a soft thump on top of his thighs as he first kneels and then sits down on the ground. She wraps her legs around him and rests her face against his shoulder, breath ragged and heart pounding in her fingertips. His arms hold her tight against him, and she can feel his pulse pounding as they sit there.

When she finally looks up at him, heart slowed to a semi-normal rhythm, he is smiling down at her.

"Why hello there," she says, not knowing what else to say.

"Hello yourself," he replies, and then he kisses her again, mouth soft and gentle, the roughness of the previous moments gone but not forgotten. When they part, she looks at his hair, seeing how her desperate grip has pulled it in wild directions. She grins sheepishly as she reaches up to pat it back into place. He catches her hand as she pushes a lock behind his ear, and pulls it to his mouth, placing a delicate kiss on the back of her hand.

"Thanks," she said, not sure if she is responding to the hand kiss or the impromptu fuck.

"Any time," he replies. He moves his legs beneath her. "While this is lovely, I need to move."

"Oh!" she exclaims. "Sorry." She gets up carefully, feeling him slip out of her as she moves. She puts her skirt to rights as he tucks himself back into his pants.

"Don't be sorry," he tells me. "That was amazing."

"It really was," she agrees, looking around. They are alone. She doesn't think anyone stumbled outside during their interlude. If they had, they hadn't noticed. It is pretty dark behind the building. "So..." she lets the words drag out, not sure what to say.

"So," he echoes, smirking as he fixes his belt.

"So I don't do this kind of thing."

"Nor I," he says with a shrug, "but there are first times for everything."

She nods. "So what's the etiquette here? Do I just say thanks and head home? Am I supposed to buy you dinner?"

He glances at his watch. "It's a bit late for dinner, but breakfast in a few hours could be tempting." He cocks his head, contemplating, and then adds, "Tell me about this home of yours."

"It's not far away," she says, unable to stop herself, unable to deny the little thrill that starts building again at the way he is looking at her.

He looks around, then reaches for her hand. "I can walk you there, if you want. I'm very interested in hearing about the things you don't normally do."

She takes his hand and leads him away from the wall and onto the main street. "I don't think you want to hear about that," she says. "I think you have ulterior motives."

"I may just want to fuck you again," he says, raising her hand to his lips in a gallant gesture, "and take my time about it this time."

"Already?" she asks, surprised. He's not an old man, but definitely older than the teenage boys who can go again and again without pausing.

"I assure you that my refractory period is minimal," he says, and she feels a jolt of pleasure at the way he uses words. "I'm eager for another chance, if you'd have me." She stares at him, at that sensual mouth that is clearly attached to an intellectual brain, and her nipples harden.

"That sounds like a great idea," she tells him, biting her lip. "My place is just a few blocks away...and I probably have something you can eat for breakfast."

"Good," he says, "I have an early morning."

"Me too," she agrees. "But tonight still has many hours left."

2

She opens the door to her place, frantically trying to recall just how messy she had left it when she went out a few hours ago. "Prepare yourself," she warns him. "I have a dog."

"I like dogs," he says and follows her inside to be greeted by Samwise, her black lab. Samwise is as happy as ever to see her again, and just as excited to meet her companion, and she wonders for a moment just how crazy she is to be bringing a complete stranger back to her home. But dogs are supposed to have a good sense of character. She watches her new friend kneel down to pet Samwise, sees how entranced her dog is with the newcomer, remembers that cock thrusting inside her, and decides she doesn't care about safety tonight. If she ends up on the news after being murdered, at least she will have had a few good orgasms first. "I'll have to take him out," she says. Her new friend stands up, reaches behind him to grab the leash from the hook on the wall, and clips it to Samwise's blue collar.

"Let's go," he says.

"Do you have a dog?" she asks, as they stroll slowly down the street.

He looks wistful, but shakes his head. "I did."

"Past tense?" she asks.

"Yeah…" He lets the word drag out, and she realizes that he is wondering how much to share, likely wondering how much she wants to know. She doesn't even know his name. She doesn't think she wants to know anything about him. She just wants the dog to go so that they could go inside and fuck again.

"Samwise is a great dog," she comments, saving him from sharing anything else. "He's good company."

"Does he mind company?" he asks, and she catches the undertone. Does she often bring strangers home?

She shrugs. "I don't think so." She looks over at him, heat streaking through her as she remembers those hands on her skin, those lips against hers. "I guess we will see how he feels about loud noises from the bedroom."

He smiles in a way that is all promise. "My dog used to sleep in the bed with me. Does he normally stay in there with you?"

She nods, pausing as Samwise finishes his business. "Yeah. But sometimes I boot him off the bed, especially if he's being a jerk and rolling all around. I don't think he'll go nuts if we kick him out tonight."

"Good," her new friend says as they head back to her house. She lets Samwise off the leash when they get inside, and he wanders off into the kitchen, losing interest in them and focusing on his food bowl.

"So," she says, staring at this sexy stranger next to her front door.

"So," he echoes, waiting for her.

"Is this the part where I offer you a drink?" she asks, floundering.

"Are you trying to get me drunk?" he comments, grinning.

"No," she answers, a grin growing on her face as the air heats up between them again. "But I have plenty of stuff to drink in the kitchen."

"Do you have ice?" he asks.

"Um...yeah," she tells him. "This isn't Greece. Why? You want a cold drink?"

He steps toward her, pushing her against the wall, hands on either side of her body as he leans in. "I had an idea of what I might do to you with some ice," he whispers. "You are so hot. I need to cool you down a little bit."

"And how would you do that?" she asks, voice low against his mouth.

He looks down the hall at the door to her bedroom, then in the other direction toward the kitchen. "Come with me." She follows him into the kitchen, and he lifts her onto the island across from the sink and the stove. She watches as he walks over to the refrigerator and presses the button on the front to get a handful of ice. Most of these he tosses casually into the sink, but he keeps one, holding it up to her as he approaches, fitting himself between her legs where she sits on the counter.

"Now," he says, trailing the piece of ice along the edge of her jaw to her mouth, a brief biting cold, and then he pulls it away, leaning back from her with an appraising glance. "Now I want to look at you," he tells her. "Take off your shirt."

She obeys, sliding the long-sleeved sweater over her head to reveal the plain white tank top beneath. She tosses the shirt behind her on the countertop. He nods, taking the ice and running it swiftly along her collarbone. She shivers, the melting water dripping down to wet the top of her tank top. Her nipples harden in anticipation. He leans in to kiss her, and she wraps herself around him, eager for more. He tugs the front of her tank top down to reveal one breast, taut nipple standing erect as he pushes down the edge of her bra. He teases her nipple with the ice, then, at her gasp, bends to replace the cold with the heat of his mouth. He sucks hard for a moment, his other hand reaching over to free her other breast, dexterous fingers caressing her naked skin. She wraps her hands around his head, pushing him to her. He pulls back, lips pursing to blow on her wet skin, sending shivers of delight across her body. "So lovely," he murmurs, then moves to suck the other nipple.

She moans, and then he stands up, slides the ice cube into his mouth, and lifts her tank top over her head. Her bra follows, sliding down her arms to be tossed casually to join the sweater behind her.

"Yes," he whispers, bending again to face her breasts, cold tongue licking and teasing as his hands press against her back. "Perfection," he says, one finger rubbing her nipple while his tongue licks the other. She leans into him, the cold against her nipples matching the heat between her legs. He looks up at her, a wicked grin, and then he kneels on the floor, his head even with the countertop, and slowly slides her skirt up over her thighs. "Now," he says, voice thick around the ice still in his mouth, "let me see what we have here." He pushes her back on the island so she leans on her elbows, looking down over the hills of her breasts to see his face between her thighs.

She marvels at the sight. *There is nothing sexier than a man looking up from between spread legs, eyes dark with intent, and mouth ready with promise.*

"Oh no," he whispers, fingers reaching out to touch her panties. "This will not do." He reaches up to find the edge of her panties and begins sliding them down her legs. "I will not have these in her way again. I want to have all of you."

As her panties slip off her legs and fall to the floor, he leans in again, fingers rubbing gently against her, a soft promise, and then his mouth, cold from the ice, but warm all the same closes over her. She hisses from the combination of hot and cold, pulling away from him unconsciously, and he grabs her hips and yanks her back toward him, his mouth meeting her with a long luscious lick from end to end. "Oh yes!" she moans, heels pressing into his shoulders.

"You like that?" he whispers against her skin, hot breath and cold tongue combining to make her squirm, his fingers rubbing up and down again her clit.

"Yes!" she tells him, pressing close against him.

"Tell me how you like it," he says, fingers sliding slowly up and down and then back and forth, to be replaced by his mouth in the same motion. He eases a finger inside her, pressing gently up, and she shudders against him, his tongue a slow steady rhythm against her clit.

"Like that!" she gasps, "Just like that!" She opens her eyes, looking down her body to see him looking at her, his glasses slightly askew on his nose, and he buries his mouth against her, his finger joined by another as he presses in and out in a maddening tempo. She tenses, body flooding with desire, and then he pushes her over the edge, and she comes shuddering against him. He pauses, but doesn't move away from her, his warm mouth still tight against her skin. After a moment, he flicks his tongue and she jerks upward, sensitive skin rebelling.

"I need—" she tries to remember words. "I need—"

That tongue moves against her again, and the whisper of breath, "You need more?"

"Too much!" she stammers. "Pause!"

He chuckles, breath still teasing her aroused skin, but he pulls away. "Pause," he agrees, getting to his feet and staring down at her as she dissolves into a puddle on her kitchen island. When she opens her eyes again, he is still watching her, a satisfied smile on his face. She manages to prop herself up on her elbows, willing life to come back into her legs, and grins at him.

"Yeah," she comments. "That was pretty awesome." She thinks of the ice in the sink, likely melted by now. "Definitely cooled me down."

"Now I suppose I'll have to get you all hot and bothered again," he muses. "I guess we should move to the bed."

3

$\mathcal{S}$he leads him to her bedroom, fingers gently cradling his, body eager but willing to be patient. Happily, there aren't too many clothes strewn about the place. She had done most of her costume changes in the bathroom, so all of the rejects are hanging haphazardly from the towel bars in there. She makes a mental note to try to get to them before he goes in there, if he goes in there, then decides it doesn't matter. It isn't like she will see him again. She doesn't need to impress him with her tidy household. She doesn't need to cook for him, or learn his habits, or meet his parents.

All she is going to do is fuck him again...and maybe again before the night is over and she has to go back to reality. The months ahead loom in front of her, and she shakes her head.

Tomorrow. She will deal with everything tomorrow.

Tonight is just for her.

She looks up at him as they near the bed, then gives him a gentle push so he sits on the edge. He grins as she kneels on the floor before him, taking one of his feet in her hands.

"These should definitely come off this time," she tells him, tugging the shoe off and tossing it gently aside. "These too," she murmurs, pulling off the other shoe and both of his socks, revealing nice feet with long toes to match those glorious pianists' fingers. She wonders idly if he plays an instrument. She takes one of his hands, moving the finger to her mouth and sucking the tip, noting the trimmed nails. Maybe. His hands are delicate. She can taste herself ever so faintly on his skin, and she kisses his palm. His other hand slips behind her head, stroking her hair and running down her neck.

She turns her attention to his shirt, those damn buttons calling her name. She pops one near the top, reveling in the inch of skin it reveals. "I have wanted to do this," she tells him, punctuating each word by tugging on a button, "since I first laid eyes on you."

He watches her, eyes burning with desire. "Were you undressing me with those eyes?" he whispers, both hands straying down her body, one holding a breast while the other slides around her hip. He leans forward, kissing her neck. She pushes his shirt off of one shoulder, revealing a finely muscled chest, smooth pale skin that says he doesn't spend much time outdoors without a shirt on. In the dim light of the room, she can see the lines of muscles she hasn't guessed at beneath the simple clothing, but should have recognized from the easy way he held her against the wall.

He is strong, biceps toned and able, a runner's body, a swimmer's body, a body that she wants to have naked underneath her as soon as possible. She kisses his neck, running her hands under his shirt and up his back, then sliding the shirt all the way off his other arm. She strokes his skin, revelling in the knowledge that tonight, just for tonight, he is all hers.

Her hands find his belt while she kisses along the line of his neck and shoulder, her fingers undoing the buckle and tugging it free from his pants. The button is next, easily coming free before she slowly unzips him, hands slow and yet still so eager as she pushes his pants aside.

"Lay back," she tells him, and he obeys, that glorious chest stretched out against the dark sheets. She takes a moment to appreciate the image of this man in her bed, knowing it will sustain her for the next few months. She tugs his pants off quickly then, sliding them down to the floor and pushing them out of the way. His boxers are next, and then she is kneeling on the floor next to her bed, taking the length of him in her hands before leaning down to lick the tip ever so gently. He lets out the tiniest sound, hips straining for more, to get closer to her.

"Now, now," she murmurs against his skin, one hand slipping down to cup the soft skin of his balls, tongue circling the tip of that glorious cock again, moving away from him as he presses toward her, keeping him at the same distance. "Patience is a virtue."

"Virtue is overrated," he mumbles, hands snaking around to press against her head, trying to tug her closer. She keeps her mouth on the end of his cock, but uses both of her hands to press his hands to the bed next to his hips.

"Not tonight," she tells him. "Tonight you're all mine, and I'm going to take my time with you." She sucks him fully into her mouth then, a few quick hard strokes up and down, enough to elicit a gasp and a groan, and then goes back to teasing the head again. "Or I could speed things up, if you prefer," she offers.

His hand runs over her head and strokes the curve of her neck and shoulder. She looks up to see him looking down at her, no doubt enjoying the same view she had enjoyed in the kitchen. "I am at your complete disposal, madam," he says cordially.

4

The professor arrives at her office the following morning, refreshed, satisfied, and ready for the new semester to begin. She is actually early, having woken up tired, but content, body languid in that way only a night of great sex can accomplish. Her new friend had gone home in the early hours, leaving without a promise to call, without words, without anything expected or lingering, except the kiss he gave her right before he left. She hadn't learned his name. It had been perfect. Perfect enough to let her wake without begrudging the early hour, enjoy her coffee with a pep in her step, and even get to campus without cursing the rush hour traffic.

She walks inside with plenty of time to print out her syllabi and walk them over to the mail room for copying. She is ready for the semester to begin on Monday. Another year teaching at Abraxus Tasker College, one half of the tiny Literature department. The school does have an entire English department devoted to rhetoric and composition, but the literature offerings have always been small, only one required class for all majors, a tiny part of their four-year program. Sometimes, she wonders if it's enough, but then she is glad to have a job teaching at all, and devotes herself to making her one chance with the students matter. She does love teaching.

Sitting down in the auditorium, she misses Jim Spenser, her old companion in the literary trenches. He retired last year, and though she knows they hired his replacement over the summer, a Dr. Jack Spelling, she hasn't met him yet. She'd been away at a conference during the hiring process, though she'd read some of his articles and been impressed. Dr. Spelling has a way of making Shakespeare relevant, and she knows that is why Abraxus hired him. She idly wonders how old he is or what he looks like. None of his articles have an accompanying picture.

Since she knows they will be working closely together, she hopes they will get along the way she did with Jim, that the newcomer will agree with her approach and not get too caught up in the English department drama. It had been tempting when she first arrived five years ago to get overwhelmed, the cacophony of forty writing professors arguing over textbooks and assignments and the importance of grammar, but Jim had guided her away from that maelstrom, and the years have proven the wisdom of that counsel.

She holds a tenure track position in a related field, of course, but at Abraxus Tasker College, English Composition and Literature are separate departments. She and Jim could make their own decisions about textbooks and syllabi and procedures without needing to conform with the rest of the English department. Such academic freedom in higher education is a privilege, and she will fight to maintain it in the coming years, hopefully with Dr. Jack Spelling at her side. She sighs, looking around the auditorium and seeing acquaintances but no real friends. She is going to miss Jim this year, his company, his old man sense of humor, and his voice of reason whispering in her ear, especially during meetings.

She settles into her seat, lifting the small table from the side and flipping it over to form her desk, readying herself to sit through the day of meetings—the beginning of semester announcements, sharing of new policies, reiteration of old information—all the usual in-service information for the Friday before classes started.

It shouldn't be too bad, she tells herself. A little meet and greet for the new hires, a little chit chat with colleagues she hasn't seen over the summer break.

She feels someone watching her as she pulls out her tablet and looks around. Normally, she would sit with Jim during these meetings, the two of them whispering or passing sarcastic notes to pass the time, but now she is alone. She doesn't find the source of the gaze and shrugs it off.

Of course, someone is watching her. They'd all just gotten back from break. Everyone is scanning faces, identifying friends and exchanging pleasantries. She does her part, not really looking around for anyone, her thoughts occupied with the to-do list for the afternoon, a few minor things to complete before classes start on Monday. She turns on her tablet, racking her brain for the wifi password that she hasn't used in three months.

The morning passes in a blur of email and updates, and the lunch break is only minutes away. She thinks she might sneak away to her office for the afternoon, deciding she has enough professional development planned for the semester that she can skip the sessions today.

She is sort of listening to the conversations as everyone stands up, but still mostly in her own head when a familiar voice calls her back to reality. She knows that voice, has heard it pleading, commanding, whispering, and promising for hours last night. "I'm sure she will, ma'am," her lover says.

She looks up from her tablet, eyes widening in horror as her dean introduces the newest member of the department. "Meet Dr. Jack Spelling," Dean Hendrickson is saying, the small woman standing next to where the professor is still sitting in her seat. Her boss looked right at her, eyeing the tablet with disapproval, knowing she hasn't been paying attention. The professor quickly stows her tablet in her bag, getting awkwardly to her feet, trying not to look at a face that she has seen make all manner of expressions unexpected in a co-worker. Dean Hendrickson gestures at Dr. Jack Spelling.

"He's in Jim's old office," she continues. The dean looks back and forth from the professor to her lover. "This is Dr. Jacoby," she introduces her. "She's right next door to you. She can show you the ropes."

"I'm looking forward to it," Jack says, his voice a promise of pleasure to come. Dr. Jacoby tries to ignore the frisson of desire that spirals up from her core at the sound.

She puts her hand out awkwardly to shake his, and as his fingers touch hers, she remembers where those hands have been, and a tiny shiver rises from between her thighs. "Nice to meet you," she says quietly. Then she remembers herself, and adds, "Have you moved in yet? Are you needing the tour or did you get your bearings already?"

That wicked smile teases the edges of his mouth, but his words are cordial enough. "I had the new faculty orientation yesterday, so I think I know where things are," he tells her. "Would you mind if I asked for guidance as things come up?"

"Not at all," she replies, turning back to the dean. One thing is certain—this is going to be an interesting semester.

5

Dr. Jacoby doesn't see Jack again until Monday evening after classes ended. It has been a hectic day spent cycling through attendance rosters and syllabi while reassuring the new students that they are in the right place. She sinks into her office chair with a sigh, removing the friendly "Ask Me!" button that she wears for the first week and hanging it on the bookshelf behind her. She kicks off her shoes beneath the desk, glad to be rid of them. She never wears uncomfortable shoes, and certainly won't do it knowing she is going to spend the day on her feet, but it is always a pleasure to take off her boots, relishing the feel of her feet free beneath the desk. She glances out the open door of the office, and seeing no one in the visible hallway, listens carefully.

No one seems to be around. It is late, after all, the last classes of the day finished up about a half hour ago, students scampering to waiting cars and faculty drifting home to waiting bottles of wine.

She logs into her computer and turns on her music player, choosing something upbeat enough to motivate her to get through at least a little bit of work before she calls it a day. Since no one is around, she turns up the volume, and soon she is typing away, happily yell-singing the words along with the music.

She has no idea how long she has been in the zone when she hears a soft noise behind her, a polite cough. She freezes, word dying on her lips as she stops. She immediately turns down the volume and slowly spins to see who is standing in the doorway.

Please don't be the dean, her mind chants, *please don't be the dean.*

It isn't the dean.

It is Dr. Jack Spelling, standing in the doorway of her office like he belongs nowhere else, and she finds herself sitting up straighter, tucking her feet beneath her chair, wondering how long he has been standing there watching her one-woman concert.

"Dr. Spelling," she manages after an awkward silence while he continues to stare at her. "Was I disturbing you? I didn't think anyone was still here."

"Do you often put on concerts after everyone goes home?" he asks, and there is that sexy lilt in his voice, and suddenly she wants him to come into her office, slam the door, and have his way with her right on top of her desk. She closes her legs, willing the image away, the papers askew on the floor, pen cup rolling away as he raises her dress...she takes a deep breath and looks away from the desk back to where he stands.

She shrugs guiltily, "Maybe?" After a pause that threatens to turn into something else, she asks, "How was your first day?"

Jack shrugs, shoulders filling out that shirt in a way that makes her want to unbutton it all over again. "The usual," he says, "syllabus, learning names, you know the drill."

She nods. "I always suck at learning names. It takes me forever."

Jack chuckles, "I have to say you suck very well, Dr. Jacoby. And I have no doubt you prove an adept learner. As for names..." He trails off, body leaning slightly more into her office than before.

She leans back in her chair, then nods her head at the seat in front of her desk, inviting him to sit. He reads her signal, stepping inside and sitting down. "I didn't think I'd ever see you again," she says bluntly. "I didn't think I needed to learn your name."

"Do you want to know it now?" he asks, and the question is filled with meaning.

She considers. Does she? It is one thing to have mind-blowing sex with a complete stranger, knowing it isn't going to last. It is another to continue to have mind-blowing sex with a co-worker that she will have to see every day. That is something she has always avoided. Maybe he has as well.

"Do you want to know mine?" she counters. He knows her last name, but her first name isn't posted anywhere at the college. Only her first initial is there: C.

He leans back in the chair, one ankle coming up to rest on his knee, his hands going behind his head. She sees that his hair is mussed, the ends wild in a curly mass around his face, and she wants to run her fingers through it again, tugging it up even more than it already is. "This could be..." he pauses, "complicated."

She nods, knowing that while there isn't a specific rule against dating co-workers, the college doesn't exactly encourage it. "It could."

"Or it could be..." he pauses again, this time a wicked smile crossing his face, "wonderful."

"Go on," she tells him, liking that grin, liking the thrill that fills her chest even more.

He puts his leg down and leans forward. "This could be exciting."

She glances behind him at the open door, hesitation draining out of her at the thought of fucking him again right there in her office. "It could," she repeats. He sees where she is looking and stands up, eyes watching her as he slowly slides the doorstop out of the way and lets the door shut firmly, leaning against it, hand cradling the handle behind his back. She stands up, walking to stand in front of him. He reaches for her instantly, long arms wrapping around her back and tugging her close for a kiss. He tastes like mint, and she pulls the gum he's been chewing into her mouth. They both stumble awkwardly backward, narrowly missing the chair to bang against her desk. He lifts her easily on to it, hands reaching down to push her dress up her thighs, fingers sliding her panties aside.

"Dr. Jacoby," he breathes into her open mouth, "you're so wet for me."

She begins unbuckling his belt, fingers clumsy in her haste, and is pleased to find him hard and ready for her. "Dr. Spelling," she tells him, stroking the length of him in both palms, "you're so hard for me."

He braces himself on the desk with one hand, the other still pressing against her flesh, and kisses her savagely, sucking her lip into his mouth and taking back the gum she'd taken from him.

"You want me?" he asks into her mouth. "You want me here, now, like this?"

"I want you," she tells him, hands pulling him close, then releasing him to grab his hips and press him between her legs. "I want you to fuck me right here on this desk."

He groans as he enters her, his hand holding her panties aside just long enough for him to slide inside, and then one hand is on her lower back, pressing her to him, and the other is on the back of her head, fingers twisting in her hair.

"Yes!" she moans into the kiss. "Fuck yes!" There is a small crash as the cup of pencils she keeps on the edge of her desk flies to the floor. She ignores it. He grabs her ass to lift her to a better angle, and then she hears nothing except their harsh breaths and the sounds of their bodies together, senses focusing on the feeling, losing herself in the pleasure as he brings her to the edge and crashing over it.

6

A week later, Dr. Jacoby is sitting in her office, shoes kicked off under the desk, brain exhausted. She hits send on the last email, and her hands fall to her lap, fingers absently rubbing along her thighs where the buckles of her garters rest. It has been a long day, but punctuated by secret thrills as a new sensation would rub against her bare flesh. She wears tights occasionally, so the material against her legs isn't foreign, but it has been a while since she wore stockings with garters. This morning, she made sure that her dress is long enough to cover everything—no need to flash students with things they have no business seeing. But now that classes are over for the day, she is lingering in her office, waiting to see if Dr. Spelling will be around. He has another class after her last one for the day, but he should be finishing up any minute now. She expects to hear his voice in the hallway soon, no doubt accompanied by a female student eager for some one-on-one time with her handsome professor. Dr. Jacoby isn't the only one to find Dr. Spelling attractive.

She waits for a little bit, just relaxing in her comfortable desk chair, letting her hands wander over her bare flesh, relishing in the naughtiness of touching herself in her office. The door is open, but no one can see her without walking inside, and she will hear them approach since she doesn't have any music on. There is little risk of discovery, but it is still fun to play at work.

She thinks of hands on her skin, fingers sliding under her dress, followed by soft butterfly kisses and the warmth of breath, and then a hot tongue against—

She hears voices down the hall, and quickly removes her hand from beneath her dress. The sound continues for a few, quiet and comfortable, a deep rumble that she knows is Dr. Spelling, a higher voice that no doubt belongs to one of his students. All of the girls find reasons to visit him during his office hours. He is charming.

But tonight, he is hers.

She waits a little bit longer, catching a word here and there, knowing that their discussion of the assignment is long over, and the student is reaching for reasons to stay. Finally, Dr. Jacoby is tired of waiting, and she knows the feeling Jack must have right now, waiting for the student to leave him alone. She always appreciates it when a colleague rescues her from a clingy student. She can do the same for Jack now.

She slides on her shoes, sensible heels this time instead of her boots, and grabs her keys, letting her office door slide shut behind her. Her heels make a light tapping sound as she walks down the hall to Jack's office. She knows he can hear her coming.

"Let me know if you have any more questions, Bree," he says as she comes into view in his doorway. He looks at her, a slow smile crossing his face, his eyes sliding up her body as Bree turns around in the chair to see who has arrived. Dr. Jacoby flashes the student her best professorial look, friendly but done for the day. She turns back to Jack, whose face is all business again. "Ah, Dr. Jacoby," he says, addressing her over Bree's head. "I had a question for you." He smiles politely at his student, but the message is clear.

Bree stands slowly, angling her body to show her cleavage and lowcut shirt as she grabs her bag from the floor by her chair. "Thanks, Dr. Spelling," she breathes. "I really appreciate it."

"Any time," he replies, and then she is walking out of the door and down the hallway.

Dr. Jacoby waits a beat, lingering in the doorway until the footsteps fade away. "Any time?" she repeats. "You're so helpful, Dr. Spelling."

He turns back to the computer situated on the short side of his L-shaped desk, clicking the mouse a few times as he finishes up some work. "Always," he assures me.

"Am I disturbing you?" she asks, stepping into his office.

"No," he says, shaking his head. "I actually did have some questions for you," he adds, shuffling through some papers on his desk, his body sideways to where she stands across from his desk. She walks over to him, stepping around the desk to the right to stand behind his chair. He gives her a quick glance over his shoulder, smirks a little, and then returns to his papers.

"What's on your mind, Dr. Jacoby?" he asks in a perfectly even tone.

"I don't know," she murmurs, running a hand through his hair and leaning down to kiss the side of his neck. "I thought I'd come harass a colleague for a bit." She nibbles a little on his skin, earning a soft sigh as he relaxes into her. "Something to pass the time between grading."

"You aren't supposed to be grading," he says quietly, one hand reaching back to stroke the line of her ass through her skirt, the other still clicking the mouse here and there as he opens and closes windows on the computer. "Not yet, anyway. And aren't these your office hours? You're supposed to be here for your students." His hand pauses as he reaches her thigh, no doubt discovering the small bump of the garters, and he spins his chair to face her, computer screen forgotten.

"I'm always here for my students," she replies, reaching down to stroke him through his pants. "Like you, I'm a dedicated professional."

"I hope you didn't wear this for your students," he says, both hands sliding up her legs and lingering on the top of her stocking, fingers stroking the bare flesh of her inner thigh. "Definitely a professional, but not in this field."

"I can't be extra helpful for my students?" she asks, unzipping his pants and reaching inside to pull out his hard shaft.

He gasps as she touches him, hands moving from under the front of her dress around to squeeze her bare bottom. "Not like this, Dr. Jacoby," he growls. "You can only be extra helpful for me."

She sinks to her knees before him, forcing him to abandon her ass. His hands settle on her shoulders. "Giving me orders, I see," she says. "I don't know if you're in a position to be giving the orders quite yet. I'm the one with seniority in this department." She breathes on the tip of his cock, watching him harden even more before her. "You should listen to me. I have some valuable institutional knowledge that will help you fit in here."

"I will never dispute your seniority in this department," he swears, face eager as he watches her, "and I hope I continue to fit in here." His hand reaches down between their bodies to cup between her legs.

"I'm glad we sorted that out," she giggles, then glances to her left where the stack of papers still sat next to his keyboard, the pile level with where her head is. "Let me guess," she says, leaning down to lick the tip of his cock as he leans back in his chair again. "Trying to fill out your office hour form?"

He moans, glances at the open door, then over at the pile she is talking about. "How did you guess?"

"It's counter-intuitive," she says, letting the word stretch out against his skin as she licks the length of him. "You'd think engineers made it or something." He chuckles, and she asks, "Did you look at the sample they sent you?"

"Sample?" he groans, leaning back farther in the chair with his eyes closed, the back pressed up hard against the edge of the desk. If she pushes him back any more, the keyboard will jam into the monitor. His hand grips the long edge of the desk to his right.

She sucks him fast, deep and hard, twice, tugging him toward her, and then releases him, sitting back on her haunches to look him over, eyebrow raised. "Did you not read your email, Dr. Spelling? What kind of employee are you?"

He chuckles again, glancing at the door once more, then at the stack of papers to his right, the top few askew where his hand has bumped them, and finally down at where she kneels before him. "The kind who teaches literature," he says, "and can't be bothered with little things like forms."

"You'd better start paying attention to little things," she admonishes, a hand reaching up to undo one of the buttons on her dress. "This is officially a STEM college, after all. They love their little details." She undoes another button, revealing the lacy top of her bra.

"Those," he says, "are not little details, Dr. Jacoby." She smiles and he bites his lip. She undoes another one. His hand reaches down to help with the next one, but she swats him away. His hand goes to his cock instead, giving himself a few quick pumps as he watches her unbutton the rest of the dress. "Lovely," he breathes, "down to the last detail."

"I am glad you approve," she says. "I want you to feel comfortable, of course."

"I'm feeling very relaxed right now," he answers.

She grins at him, then leans down to take that cock in her mouth again. "I am part of the welcome committee," she says against his skin.

"Does everyone get such a welcome?" he asks.

She looks up at him, his cock in her mouth, then slowly licks the tip. "Oh no," she says. "This is a special occasion."

"It definitely is," he breathes.

"Now," she says, reaching into his pants to cup his balls, "you are going to fill out that form."

"You can help me later."

"I am helping you now," she says, giving him a squeeze, "and you will do it now."

He smirks, then reaches for the stack of papers. He pulls out the yellow form in question, placing it on top of the pile. "And if I do?"

"Then I will see if you've done it properly, gotten all those details in the right place," she tells him, lazily swirling her tongue around him.

"And if I have?"

"Then I will have to have this cock in my pussy while I look it over," she promises, sucking him deep again, keeping her head below the level of the desk just in case someone walks by in the hallway. He groans, and she hears the shuffling of paper and pen as he fills out the form. She keeps up a delicious rhythm, enough to get him excited, but not enough for him to come. She wants way more action tonight before they are through. After a few moments, the pen hits the desktop, and she looks up at him.

"It's done," he says, face red with excitement, the flush disappearing into his collar. She reaches up and unbuttons his shirt, pushing it away from his chest, following that heat down his belly and along that delicious muscle right above his cock. She pulls his pants and boxers down, pushing him back onto the chair, then turning them both around to face the computer. She settles herself on his lap, his hands holding her ass, that hard cock pressing into her, sliding inside so easily, and she sinks into the feeling for a moment before remembering herself. His hands slip around her hips, reaching up to caress her breasts as she moves slowly up and down. He kisses her neck, squeezes her nipples, and she almost forgets why she is there.

"Dr. Jacoby," he whispers against her skin.

"Yes," she moans, moving up and down again, his cock pressing in all the right ways inside her.

"How did I do?"

"You're doing fine," she mumbles, picking up the rhythm as she splays her fingers flat on the desk in front of her, using it to push up and down faster.

"The form," he murmurs against her neck. "How is the form?"

She reaches around blindly to grab the yellow paper and scans the form briefly, seeing that he actually has filled it in properly—she's seen many people put the wrong information in the wrong spot—then she stops, stands up, turns around to face him, wraps her legs around him, and slides that cock back inside her, her breasts pressing against his bare chest.

He moves her faster, hands lifting her and tugging her to him for a passionate kiss. "Perfect form," she whispers against his lips as the slow burn spins up from her belly, "as always, Dr. Spelling."

7

"Don't forget to read all of the Dickinson poems for next time, plus the bio," Dr. Jacoby announces, glancing at the clock a final time. "And there's a quiz online. Please take it before you come to class next week," she adds, raising her voice slightly to be heard over the sudden shuffle of notebooks closing and zippers opening. The class empties slowly, students waiting on one another to continue conversations as they leave. She busies herself at the computer up front, gathering up her folders, shuffling papers into manageable piles, brain running through her after class checklist.

She is fairly certain she covered everything she meant to. She collects the few sticky notes she had jotted concepts on, checking each one off the mental roster she has for the class— Poe, Virginia, "Annabel Lee," "the Raven," Baltimore, Election Day—when a soft shuffle catches her attention. She looks up, expecting to see a student with a question, and is rewarded with a handsome Dr. Spelling instead. He stands just inside the doorway, the last student having left and the door closing with a soft thump. He cocks his head and looks her over, a slow grin crossing his face.

"Dr. Jacoby," he says, "you look good enough to eat."

She blushes, leaning down and resuming her piling— graded assignments on the bottom, then notes from today, then the homework they just turned in, and then attendance sheet on top. She needs to keep things straight as she stacks them or she'll never figure out what assignment belonged where. "And are you hungry, Dr. Spelling?" she asks, straightening her pile and looking up to drink him in.

His shirt is dark today, the top button at the collar undone since he is probably done teaching for the day. It is still tucked into his pants, the dark leather of his belt visible. She catches the slight bulge of his crotch and lets her eyes wander slowly back up to his face, letting him watch her appreciation. His hair is a bit wild, like it always is by the end of the day, the effect of running his hands through it as he taught. She thinks it must make his students laugh, the dark curls nearly standing on end after hours of classes. She wants to run her hands through it now.

He walks down the aisle between the tables to the front of the room where she stands, leaning against the front row and tilting his head. "I'm always hungry for you," he whispers, the words making her shiver.

She glances at the door, the small glass rectangle showing the hallway beyond clearly. The lights are still on out there, meaning that someone is still moving around and triggering the motion-sensor lights, but she can't see anyone out there. The building will empty out at this time, but there can still be a few students wandering around, searching for professor's offices or for other students. They aren't nearly alone, not like when they meet in their offices. She looks at where he leans against the table, the two chairs on the far side, and a naughty idea begins to form. It is risky, though. Much riskier than anything else they've done.

He seems to follow her thoughts, eyes moving from her to the lectern which stands a few feet from him, up from the floor on a small elevated podium. She rarely uses it, preferring to move around and lead discussions, but every classroom has one.

"So, I've been encouraged to visit some classrooms," Dr. Spelling says conversationally, "to observe my colleagues and their teaching style."

"Is that right?" she asks, making a face. "Does the dean expect you to start lecturing like the rest of the tech people?"

He shrugs, those gorgeous shoulders lovely to behold as he moves. "Maybe?" He frowns. "Is that how we're supposed to do it here?"

She shakes her head. "No. Absolutely not. We're Literature people, Dr. Spelling. We generally have discussions and conversations about the reading. We aren't teaching someone how to code, or how to take an x-ray," she says, mentioning some of the other programs at the college. "We teach a general education course. Our job is to teach them how to think."

"Is that what general education is about?" he asks, raising one of the core questions in their discipline, a conversation she's had at many meetings, defending the arts to people who valued numbers and hard evidence. "Teaching them what to think?"

"Oh no," she replies, walking toward him, catching the shift in his question, the same trap many of the AS—Associate of Science—faculty would use, "not *what* to think—*how* to think." She shrugs. "We teach critical thinking skills, and that takes practice, and practice for us means discussion." She reaches out to take his hand, loving the heat that moves through her as their skin meets. She gives him a serious look. "Don't feel like you have to lecture here because that's how most of the classes are."

He brings her hand up to his lips, kissing it. "How do the students respond?" he asks. "Do they expect lectures?"

She nods, watching his mouth. "Sure! But they tend to open up once we start discussing the reading. You'd be surprised how much they get into it, even the poetry, once you let them know it's okay to relax and talk about it." She pauses, reading the face of a concerned colleague questioning his craft. "Why? Did they give you grief about something?"

"No," he says, tilting his head to the side, "not really. But they were definitely surprised."

"Why?" she asks, hopping onto the table to sit next to him.

He shrugs. "I recited some Shakespeare for them, and they were shocked that I had it memorized."

She nods, letting their still clasped hands fall to his thigh. "No doubt. Did they ask why you bothered?"

He laughs, "Not in so many words, but yes."

"They don't tend to value knowledge that isn't clearly practical here, not at first. That's what I spend most of my time teaching them—that it's okay to learn about something for its own sake—that knowledge doesn't have to have an immediate, practical use," she explains. She looks at him. "What poem did you recite?"

"The usual," he says, "'Shall I compare thee.'"

"I like that one." She squints at him, mouth curling up playfully as she slides her hand up his thigh. "Did you tell them it's about a guy? They tend to get thrown when I mention that."

He chuckles, his hand drifting to her thigh and stroking the outside. "No. I don't want to cause waves during my first few weeks here by explaining pederasty." He pauses, hand resting firmly against her, separated by the material of her skirt. "I focused on the words. I think they enjoyed the 'fair from fair' bit once I explained it."

"I love that part," she agrees, "and who wouldn't want to always remain lovely and desirable throughout time?" He winks at her, hands giving her a quick squeeze, and she stumbles back into work mode. "Do you usually read it from the book or do you recite it from memory?" she asks.

"Memory," he shrugs again, hand retreating back to touch the outside of her thigh. "I have a lot of Shakespeare in my brain."

"Occupational hazard," she admits. "I did Poe today, and I've done it so many times that I can recite 'The Raven' without looking down at the page." She looks at him, trying to rekindle the mood and knowing just how to do it. "How did you recite it?"

He looks at her, confused. "What do you mean?"

"Like, did you stand up front and bust out with it, or did you set it up on the overhead, or did you walk around and say it...?"

"I just stood up front and said it."

She smirks, letting her hand wander again. "I bet the girls loved that."

He laughs, leaning back a little to give her better access. "What? Why?"

She gives him a look, hand pressing against his cock through his pants. "It's a love poem, recited by a sexy professor. I bet most of the girls are drooling over you by the end of class."

"But will you be drooling over me, Dr. Jacoby?"

"I don't know," she says teasingly. "I'd have to hear it first."

"Seriously?"

She nods, removing her hand and leaning back on her elbows on the table, her skirt riding up to reveal more of her stockings than she ever shows in class. "Oh yes," she says dramatically, "Recite some Shakespeare for me, Dr. Spelling."

He smiles, and she can see him relishing the words as he speaks. "Shall I compare thee to a summer's day?" he begins, gesturing at her. "Thou art more lovely and more temperate..."

She sits up and clasps her hands at her chest, wowed by him even as he speaks the words she knows so well. She has always been a sucker for poetry, even back in high school. She may have specialized in American Literature, but she never lost her love of the Bard.

He glances behind them at the doorway, and seeing nothing, leans down, words decreasing to a whisper as he speaks against her lips, "and every fair from fair sometimes declines," he says, and then he is kissing her, and she runs her fingers through his hair. The kiss breaks after a moment, and he continues, hands moving down her sides and under the seam between her shirt and skirt to touch the bare skin of her midriff. "But thy eternal summer shall not fade," he murmurs against her chin, one hand reaching up to tilt her neck to the side and brush her hair aside so he can kiss the skin there, "nor lose possession of that fair thou ows't...". He finishes the words, leaving her breathless with lust and aching with desire.

"That was..." she begins, trying to find words between the pulsing rush of desire in her skin, "that was lovely." She takes a moment, breathing heavily, stirred by the depth of her response to him. "I hope you didn't deliver it in class like that," she says finally. She wants him to take her right there on the table, but he steps away from her, looks from her to the lectern and back again, face calculating.

"Oh no," he assures her, stepping up onto the podium. "I stood up here and said it."

She smiles and shakes her head. "I never stand up there."

He hops down and takes a few steps toward her. "Why not?"

She shrugs, letting him tug her off the table to her feet. "I don't know. I'm not a lecturer like that. It just doesn't seem to work."

"What doesn't work?" he asks. "Let me see you up there."

She obliges, humoring him, stepping up and behind the lectern, leaning her hands against the slanted top, gazing out at the classroom. "I'm supposed to stand here," she tells him, "and talk." She turns around to gesture at the white board behind her. "Though I don't know why anyone would. I can't even reach the board from here. I couldn't write anything down."

He approaches, stepping up behind her and wrapping his arms around her middle. She leans back into his embrace, letting herself relish the feel of him, the smell of him, his heat so close through his clothes. She molds her body to his, pressing back and feeling the stirrings of delicious hardness behind her.

"But Dr. Jacoby," he whispers in her ear, and she shivers, "others use PowerPoint presentations to teach. They don't write on the board."

She rolls her eyes. "They also use the same presentation from ten years ago," she mutters. "They can recite it in their sleep at this point."

He nods, sliding around to face her, wedging himself between her and the lectern. She glances at the door, seeing shapes moving by in the hallway, but no one opens the door and comes inside. She looks up at him, his face only a few inches above her own. "Can you recite it?" he whispers.

"Recite what?"

"Your lesson," he says, leaning down to trail small kisses down her neck and across her shoulder, tugging her sweater down as he does so. "You covered Poe today."

"You want to hear my lesson on Poe?" she asks, a bit breathless.

"I want to hear your recite some Poe," he says, hands reaching down to her thighs and sliding up under her skirt. He lingers on the stockings she nearly always wears now, then lets his hands slip up farther, stroking her clit with a forcefulness that makes her gasp, "under duress."

Her knees grew weak as he continued to press against her, heat and wetness building in her lower belly. "What kind of duress?" she squeaks, as he gives her a wicked grin, turns around to glance at the door, turns back to her, winks, and kneels before her, body hidden from view by the lectern. His hands slide around to cup her ass, and then he is lifting her skirt and ducking underneath it, his mouth meeting her clit with a long, succulent kiss. Her legs jolt and she nearly falls against him, hands pressing hard into his shoulders. "Oh god!" she moans, pleasure streaking through her.

"That's not the first line." His voice drifts up, his breath hot on her skin, his fingers sliding up her inner thighs to press against the edges of her opening.

"Please," she begs, wanting him to lick her again.

"That's not the first line, either," he replies, and he kisses the top of her thigh instead. "Focus, Dr. Jacoby."

"Once…" she says, letting the word trail off as he kisses her clit again, warm sparks shooting up into her lower belly. But then his mouth is gone. Waiting.

She ransacks her brain for the lines of poetry she knows by heart. She can do this. She deserves this. She knows this poem inside and out. She can totally do this.

"Once upon a midnight dreary," she begins, words sure and strong. She is rewarded by another long, wet kiss, followed by a strong finger slipping inside her.

"Yes…" he moans against her, encouraging, and she shudders.

"While I pondered," she continues, "weak and weary," and there is another of those licks, this time keeping rhythm with her words. "Over many a quaint and curious volume of forgotten lore," she says quickly, the words tripping over one another in her haste to get them out, and she is rewarded by solid sucking and another finger joining the first. She presses down on his shoulders, needing him to continue. "While I nodded," she says, and then he is nodding against her, his chin pressing into her lips and his tongue working magic against her clit, and those fingers rubbing in and out, in and out, "nearly napping," she breathes, and then there is a third finger, and she is nearly riding his hand now, one hand death gripping his shoulder and the other pressing him against her through the fabric of her skirt. "Suddenly, there came a tapping," she wheezes, and his fingers began a maddening rhythm that make her legs begin to shake, "as of someone gently rapping," she breathes, "rapping at my chamber door," she manages, and closes her eyes, sinking into the feeling, pressing herself into him. She is almost there when he pauses, breath hot against her as he says, "That's not the entire poem, Dr. Jacoby."

The fingers abandon her, leaving her feeling hollow and aching, and he pauses, face an inch away from where she wants him. She slides her skirt up around her belly, looking down at him, seeing his face where he kneels before her, his hair a wild mass of curls in every direction. She grabs a handful and presses him back against her, but he grabs the back of her skirt and tugs, pulling her away from him.

"Oh no, Dr. Jacoby," he says, "you'll have to do better than that."

She rallies, her brain trying to conjure the words while the aching builds. "Umm.." she says, stalling for time, "umm..." His hands slide up the back of her thighs, cupping her ass, thrilling but not the thrill she wants at the moment. "Tis some visitor!" she nearly shouts, the words coming to her in a rush. She is rewarded with another of those long kisses, his tongue licking long, his lips sucking hard. "Some late visitor entreating entrance at my chamber door," she continues in a rush, but at the word "door," she realizes that she has had her eyes closed again. She glances quickly at the door, seeing shapes in the hallway, but none near the glass. She hopes no one had walked by and peered in. She glances down at Jack's head buried in her crotch and pleasure jolts through her again, the thought of being caught at any moment an unexpected thrill along with the challenge of reciting poetry. "Only this," she finishes quickly, focusing on the building warmth and rising wave, "and nothing more!" At the final word, he slips three fingers inside her again, the rhythm enough to make her come almost immediately. She shudders against him, breathing hard, seeing stars, and then sags against the lectern, leaning over him.

He chuckles, his breath warm against sensitive skin, and she jerks away, needing a moment. His hands retreat a safe distance to cup her ass again, and he chuckles again. "I need to see that ass," he orders, getting to his feet and spinning so the lectern was behind them. He lifts her easily, placing her on the edge of the lectern, her clit and vagina easily accessible. She tries to glance behind her at the door, but his hand is stroking her again, and she closes her eyes instead. "Yes…" she moans, and then he is pulling her slightly closer, throwing her legs over his shoulders and leaning forward.

"I want to see you squirm, Dr. Jacoby," he says, sliding closer to her, tugging her closer for another long kiss and suck of her clit and lips, "and I want to feel all of you," he says, and then his hands are under her, fingers sliding inside her with a sweet jolt, and his other hand lifting her even more into the air. She squeezes against his fingers, loving the feeling, and he leans forward for another long sucking kiss that has her shuddering against him. His fingers begin to move and she loses herself, coming hard again. "Oh, yes," he chuckles, moving one leg down from his shoulder to his waist, where it hangs limply, but leaving the other on his shoulder, looking intently at her.

"Hmm?" she asks dreamily.

"All this talk of chamber doors," he murmurs, "and here I thought we'd never get there." At this, his fingers begin slowly moving toward her ass. "Are you into other doors, Dr. Jacoby?" he whispers, leaning forward to give her another quick lick as his fingers explore deeper inside her.

"I don't know if Edgar Allan Poe would approve," she murmurs, "but I'm with Shakespeare on this one. I'm open to all doors." His finger slips inside her then, slow and careful, using the wetness of his mouth and her excitement to lube the way.

She sighs, leaning down into his hand, and then he is licking her again, bringing her to the edge with sudden efficiency, and when she comes, he slips two fingers inside and she shudders against him.

"Again?" he whispers against her sensitive skin, but her legs are throbbing with fatigue and she needs to move. She shakes her head, bringing her legs down to the floor and sliding off the lectern. "I need you inside me," she says, all thought of discovery lost in her lust.

"Inside you where?" he asks, spinning her so he stands behind her. He steps off the podium, the few inches putting her ass at the perfect height for him. He undoes his belt quickly, positioning himself behind her, his hard length pressing against her opening. She is soaking wet from his mouth and her own excitement, so she doesn't think she will even need lube. He pulls her hard against his chest, kissing her neck, hands caressing her breasts under her shirt, reaching into her bra to squeeze her taut nipples. "Where do you want me inside you, Dr. Jacoby?" he whispers.

She glances at the door, noting that the hallway lights have gone out. No one has walked by in at least five minutes. The lights will turn on again if anyone does, their movement tripping the motion sensor in the hallway, though she wonders if either of them would even notice. She decides that she doesn't even care. "I want you to fuck me in the ass," she says, turning her head to see his face, her eager mouth claiming his lips, tasting him as he drives his tongue into her mouth.

"I thought you'd never ask," he says against her mouth, and then he is rubbing himself with her slickness, pressing the head of his cock against her opening, and he slides ever so slowly inside. She leans back hard against him, using gravity to help her slide onto him, his cock filling her in new ways. She reached the bottom of his cock, and then he lifts her ever so gently, letting her slide back down again. She moans and moves again, getting a rhythm going. She uses the height difference to her advantage, putting her full weight on her legs and feet as she moves on him, and his hands slip from cradling her ass to rub her clit again, his thumb sliding against her in the perfect pressure, and soon she is shuddering against him, the feeling of fullness echoing through her entire body.

"What do you think of the lectern now, Dr. Jacoby?" he asks, moving inside her, letting the moment build again.

"Quite delightful, Dr. Spelling," she breathes, sliding down his cock again. "You make me rethink my position on lecturing."

"I hope to discover all manner of positions with you," he replies, moving faster now, pushing up as she presses back. "Though this is definitely one of my favorites."

"It was the poetry," she admits, bracing herself against the lectern and moving even faster now. "I can't resist a good performance."

He presses himself deep inside her again, his thumb beginning that slow sweet stroking against her clit. "Is it good?" he asks, breathing hard as his own climax draws near.

"So fucking good," she answers, leaning back and finding his mouth with hers. "I find your performative skills to be quite enthralling!" And then she is coming hard and so is he, and they forget about words for a time.

8

*D*r. Jacoby shifts in her desk chair, trying to figure out how to get the student sitting across from her to take the hint and leave her alone. Not that she minds talking to students, she doesn't at all, but he's been in her office for forty minutes already, she has emails piling up and forms to turn in before she heads home tonight, and she needs to catch the dean before she leaves for the day to sign off on her travel paperwork.

"Of course," she nods, "that's another one of the great things about Dickinson's poetry." Her end of the conversation has been reduced to agreement in the last few minutes, but he doesn't seem to get the hint. She turns her body away from him a little bit more so she's nearly facing the computer to her left, obviously clicking on an email and scanning it. "We can always get more from it each time we read it," she finishes absently, mouse clicking as she scrolls down the message.

William still sits in the chair across from her, leaning forward, face eager to continue the discussion. He is a good kid, she knows that, good looking too, but she doesn't have time for this kind of drawn-out discussion today. *Now, if I didn't spend so much time fucking my colleague...* her mind observes sarcastically, but she shuts it down, skimming another email and deleting it.

"But what about—?" He begins anew, and she has to shut this down.

"I'm so sorry, William," she says bluntly, since he isn't catching any of her subtle hints to leave. "I have a ton of work to finish, and I have to turn this in before I leave today," she gestures at the computer screen, where her travel paperwork has finally opened, taking up most of the monitor. "I'd love to continue this chat, but another time."

"Oh, yeah!" he says, embarrassed and flustered as he starts gathering his bag. "Of course," he agrees, getting to his feet awkwardly. "Sorry to bother you."

"You're not bothering me," she reassures him, "not usually! I just have to get this done now." She smiles at him, then realizes she can see the small bulge of a semi-erection as he stands, and she looks quickly away, trying to forget the image. She tries never to think of her students that way.

Once, she had a terribly wicked dream about a current student and she had never been able to look him in the eye again. It was unfortunate because he was a great student, and she would have enjoyed more conversations with him, but she couldn't get the dream out of her head. Every time she saw him, her cheeks flamed with the memory. Why couldn't she be like some of the other faculty members who were perfectly willing to have sex with students? She can understand hooking up with a former student after the class is over—people meet lovers in all sorts of situations—but there are a few of her colleagues who are not so moral. She definitely has a problem with that.

She looks at William, knowing she could never bring herself to sleep with him, cute smile or not, sees the bulge again, and then she tries not to think of what William's cock would look like at full mast, how it would feel in her mouth. She nods at him, smiling brightly, feeling heat creep up her chest, "Have a good one, William," she says. "I'll see you next time."

"Sure!" he agrees. "Good luck with your paperwork."

And then he is gone, and the hallway is silent, and she is hard at work again. After a frantic thirty minutes, she thinks she might be finished. After another eight minutes, she has scanned the document for the last time. She has just pressed the print button when movement in her doorway has her glancing in that direction.

"Dr. Spelling," she smiles, always glad to see him. "How nice of you to drop by."

He smiles back, looking at the sea of sticky notes across her desk, "Am I disturbing you? I can come back another time."

She shakes her head, starting to gather them up, balling up the completed tasks with relish and tossing them into the recycling bin. "Actually, no. I just finished." She glances at the clock on the wall. "And I have exactly twenty-one minutes to get this to the dean's office for her signature."

"Nicely done," he congratulates. "Twenty-one minutes. That's not a lot of time."

"Isn't it, though?" she asks, her eyes inviting, and she gestures for him to come inside. "Shall we see how much we can accomplish in a few minutes?" He nods, moving to sit in the student chair, but she shakes her head, a wicked thought forming. "No," she tells him, "come here." She slides the rest of the papers from the small desk in front of her to her left so they sit on the computer desk instead, then picks up the cup of pencils, gives him a meaningful look, and places it on the bookshelf behind her. She's been finding random pencils on the floor for weeks now.

She adjusts her chair, letting her weight push it to the lowest setting so she is much closer to the floor, and gestures at the empty desk in front of her. "Sit."

He obeys, stepping around the desk to sit on top of it, his knees spreading so she can scoot her chair between them. "What's this?" he asks, glancing at the travel paperwork on top of the pile she just moved. "Going somewhere?"

"The International Shakespeare Conference," she tells him, hands reaching forward to touch him, wrapping around his back and tugging him forward a few inches. "I wanted to talk to you about it." She moves her hands down, unbuckling his belt as she speaks.

"Oh?" he asks. "I like talking to you." He moves his hands to rest on the table next to his hips, bracing himself as she opens his pants. "I also like when you do things like this." He closes his eyes for a moment, then rallies, returning to the conversation, "Your proposal?"

"They accepted it," she tells him, moving on to his button and zipper. "It's not until the summer, but I wanted to get the funding sorted out now before it's all gone."

She has his pants open, and she reaches in to pull out his cock, pleased as always to see how hard he already is for her. "Are you going this year?" she asks, then leans forward to take him into her mouth, relishing the hardness, loving how much joy this cock brings her. She leans back, releasing him, "I know you submitted a proposal."

He looks down at her, excitement at such a warm welcome on his face, "I am going," he says, then gasps as she draws him deep inside her mouth.

She releases him with a long pop. "Congratulations," she tells him, smile spreading on her face. "So we'll both be there... together."

The word hangs between them, and she leans down to suck him again, but he puts a hand under her chin, lifting her face to look at her.

"Do you want to go...together?" he asks, face hopeful.

"Do you?" she asks instead, not wanting to misunderstand his intentions. They have been fucking regularly for months now, but they haven't discussed a relationship, or the future, or anything like that.

Before he can answer, there is a noise in the hallway, a step, and then he is sliding off her desk, hands frantically trying to put his cock back inside his pants. There isn't enough time for him to fasten his pants before the visitor walks by, or even worse, walks in, so he dives under her desk instead, landing with a thump that Dr. Jacoby covers by loudly moving her chair back and then forward again. She scoots under the desk, the sides of the chair just clearing the desk surface as the person enters her office. Dr. Jacoby turns to take a drink from her water bottle, the drink giving her a moment to gather herself before she has to speak.

"Hello, Dr. Jacoby," the dean says, taking a seat across from her. "I hoped to find you still here."

Dr. Jacoby schools her face, trying not to think about the man hiding beneath the desk in front of her. "Dean Hendrickson," she begins, "I was going to come see you in a few minutes, actually."

"Call me Mary," the dean says, "No need to be formal."

"Okay Mary," Dr. Jacoby repeats, then hastily adds, "call me Celia." They share a smile, and then Celia turns slightly to scan her desk for the travel paperwork she casually tossed aside a few moments before, careful not to move her chair in case she hits Jack. She finds it, picks it up, and slides it across the desk to where the dean sits. "I have my travel packet for the Shakespeare conference this summer. I thought I would get it turned in sooner rather than later."

Celia leans forward, letting her legs and feet slip slowly down from where they have been curled up on the chair. She feels hands gentle against her feet, then they rest on both ankles, reassuring.

The dean leans forward and picks up the papers, eyes scanning them quickly. Celia uses the moment of distraction to put a hand on her lap, and a second later, Jack's warm hand is on top of it, solid and comforting. She feels her pounding heart beginning to slow, and she focuses on her boss. She knows that she and Jack have been flirting with discovery for months now, but nothing has been quite so close as this one. She tries to ignore the frisson of desire that rushes through her at the thought of the situation, Jack trapped under her desk with the dean feet away, only hidden by the wood of her desk, but she can't. Jack's hand slowly abandons hers and she brings it back up to the top of the desk. There is a moment when she can't feel him at all, and then a hand touches her calf, warm and familiar.

The dean is nodding in approval, "Yes," she says, scans something on the third page, then flips back to the top sheet, "Very nice. Perfectly done as usual." She looks up at Celia. "I can sign these here and then you can just interoffice them over to Millie at District."

"Great!" Celia agrees, then scans her desk for a pen. The cup of pencils behind her is the first thing she thinks of, so she spins the chair to retrieve them, thumping Jack in the process. There is a sharp intake of breath, which she covers with a sudden cough, hoping the dean hasn't noticed. She turns back more slowly, mindful of the man under her desk, and slides the cup across the desk to the dean. She is glad to see that a pen has found its way into the cup amid the random pencils.

The dean glances behind and around Celia's seat to the bookshelf, then at the cup. "That's an interesting place to keep your pencils," she observes, plucking the pen and beginning to sign.

"I keep knocking them over," Celia says without thinking, and then feels the blush work its way up her neck.

The dean pauses between signature and date, face curious as she takes in the simple desk, the reasonably sized office. "Are you typically rough on your desk?"

A snort works its way out before she can stop it, but she turns it into a self-deprecating chuckle. "I'm clumsy," she admits. "I'm always knocking things over with my bag when I leave." The dean nods, then turns her attention back to the papers. Celia stiffens suddenly, a quick breath turning into a soft cough, as a finger, soft and tentative, slides up from her calf and slips up to touch the bare skin of her inner thigh.

"That I can understand," the dean says, finishing her writing, and sliding the papers back over to Celia. "By the time I leave for the day, I'm too exhausted to see anything on my desk."

"I hear you," Celia says, nodding, trying not to let her face show that anything untoward is happening beneath the desk. The finger has been joined by others, and Jack's hand is slowly creeping up to stroke the tender flesh at the center of her thighs. She twists in the chair, moving her legs together, catching his hand between her thighs. "Some evenings I'm too tired to think about anything. It's like my brain reaches max capacity and shuts down."

The dean is nodding, still sitting, clearly not ready to leave yet. "And no wonder," she says, "with such a brain. Congratulations on being accepted for the conference. You may be a small department, but you're doing great things. We're grateful to have you!"

"Thanks!" Celia says, honestly touched by the praise, and trying not to think about the other places where she is being touched. The fingers have begun a slow slide back and forth within the trap of her thighs, tips grazing sensitive skin with each pass. "I'm grateful to be here!"

The dean leans forward, and Celia knows that whatever she is about to say is the real reason for her visit. "And Dr. Spelling?" she asks. "How is he settling in here?"

"Perfectly!" she replies, relaxing a bit as the hand stops moving, no doubt surprised to hear his name enter the conversation. "He's a great colleague."

"And I understand that he will also be attending the Shakespeare conference this summer," the dean says, clearly leading up to something. Celia adjusts again in the seat, and both of Jack's hands end up on the outside of her thighs, pressing against her skin.

Celia nods.

The dean gives her a look. "You know?" She raises an eyebrow. "Did he tell you today? He just told me earlier."

Celia nods again, brain trying to work out the timeline, "Yes, a few minutes before you got here. He was heading out for the evening."

"Are you two often chatting at the end of the day?"

Celia tries not to read into the question, knows that the dean is just asking the normal questions for a new faculty member, but she can't ignore the hands on her skin, the warm breath that has joined them, hot against her knees. She nods at the dean. "Sure! He's pretty great. And I know the students love him."

"Good," the dean says, "great to hear." She pauses, then takes a breath, clearly deciding to just say something. "I was thinking... since both of you are going to the same conference."

Celia cocks her head, waiting for the question though she is pretty sure where this is going. The travel budget for the school is small. Larger departments often share accommodations during travel, men and women bunking together. Celia knows that she can say no, since she would be sharing with a man, and that's why the dean has come to ask her first, to see if maybe they can half the cost of the hotel room for the week. But she waits, letting the dean ask it. The breath on her knees has moved closer, and she opens her legs a little, letting the hands slip to stroke her inner thighs again.

"Would you be willing be share a hotel room with Dr. Spelling for the trip? Have you two gotten that friendly?" The dean gives her a serious look. "No pressure, Celia. You can say no. It's absolutely fine. But I thought that you two might have grown...closer...so I thought I'd ask."

ALI WHIPPE

Celia wonders just how much the dean knows and decides not to ask. The fingers move farther up her legs, and she squirms just a little, wanting him to continue the torture but also wanting to focus on the conversation.

She pauses, appearing to consider the offer for a long moment. Does she want to share a room with Jack Spelling? Absolutely. But does he want to share a room with her? They haven't discussed such possibilities, though the eager hands on her skin suggest that he may be in favor. Eventually, she nods, "That would be fine with me. I like Jack. We get along really well. It's fine with me as long as it's fine with him."

Celia is rewarded by hot breath against her inner thighs and two fingers slide against the center of her.

"Great," the dean says. "Excellent. I'm glad everything is working out up here."

"Definitely," Celia breathes as the fingers begin a slow slide in and out of her.

"I'm glad we had this chat," the dean tells her, then stands up. Celia slides forward a few inches in her chair, and the fingers move away to give her space.

"Me too," Celia agrees, then reaches for the paperwork. "I'll get this over to Millie right away."

"Perfect. I'll talk with Dr. Spelling about this tomorrow and we can get everything settled for the conference." The dean takes a look around the office, smiles at Celia, and turns to go. "Enjoy the rest of your evening," she says.

Celia is ready to reply, but then a warm tongue licks her, and any parting words she has in mind disappear. She makes a dismissive agreeable sound instead, and then the dean is leaving, the sound of her feet echoing down the hallway. The tongue continues its motion, and Celia sits in her chair, legs frozen between terror and pleasure, sinking further into desire. After a moment, there are no more footsteps, and they are alone. Celia slides her chair back, and Jack comes with her, lifting her skirt, face staring up at her from where he still sits on the floor.

"We get along very well, do we," he begins, then adds, "Celia?" She smirks, knowing that she has never actually told him her first name. The placard on her office door just has her first initial: Dr. C Jacoby. "Why didn't you tell me?" he whispers against her skin.

She squirms against him, heart filling with more than just liquid desire. "Come on," she says, "you know why. I can only imagine what you're thinking, you Shakespeare scholar." He grins, then leans in to lick her again. "Celia is supposed to be the ungettable get," she tells him, the perfect unattainable goddess," she pauses as he kisses her again, waves of pleasure echoing through her, "the bitch who sends back flowers," she adds with a smirk, referring to the famous poem about Celia and her refusal to accept the speaker's advances, and he chuckles, the sound vibrating against her in delightful ripples.

"I'm not disputing the goddess part," he says, words poised between luscious licks, "and I would love to send you flowers, and be thrilled if you accepted them, though I will also understand if you send them back, smelling only of you," he says, referring to the rest of the famous poem. He stops, then gets up on his knees to give her a real look, dragging the chair closer so his face is level with hers. "And I'm so honored to have 'gotten' you," he adds, leaning close to give her a slow sensual kiss. She can taste herself on his lips, and she presses close, relishing the feel of him touching her, her hands winding in his hair.

"Take me then," she tells him, sliding forward in the chair, and reaching to pull him free of his pants again. He looks over his shoulder at the door, listens for a second, then turns back to her with a wicked grin, tugging the chair close by grabbing the arm rests and sheaths himself in a swift motion. Celia moans, biting her lip. He slides the chair back a few inches, then pulls her back to him, using the wheels to his advantage, setting a rhythm that has her writhing against him, legs hooked around his hips and urging him on. "Come for me!" he demands, "Come on my cock!" and then she is shuddering against him, legs locking to hold him close as their bodies shudder in unison. They hover for a long moment, their shaking breaths the only sound, and then he slides her away slowly, slipping out of her and sagging to sit on the floor in front of her. His hands drop from the armrests to her hips, and he rests his face against her thigh.

"Amazing," he breathes. "My Celia."

"Your Celia," she agrees, and he gets slowly to his knees again, folding her into a long, passionate kiss.

"Are we doing this then?" she asks when the kiss breaks and they are looking at one another openly, honestly. "Really doing this?"

He nods, face eager. "It's only been a few months, but I want more of this. I want more of you." He looks around the office. "And I want you in other places."

She cocks her head at him, confused. "Like the floor?" she asks, and he laughs.

"No!" He considers, then says, "Well, actually, yes, the floor would be lovely, but I mean that I want to see you outside of this place, outside of work, in public."

"You mean like a date?"

He nods. "Yes. I want to go out with you, spend even more time talking with you, and then bring you home and fuck you silly."

Celia smiles, "Sounds like a date to me."

"And I can't wait to go to the conference with you this summer. Together."

"And you're okay with mixing business and pleasure?" she asks, hope burning in her chest.

He kisses her again, long and slow, and the floor starts to look more and more promising. "Spending time with you is always a pleasure, whether it's business or not," he says. "I want you."

"And I want you," Celia breathes, fingers gripping him tightly. "But are you sure you will still want me this summer?"

He smiles at her, "My dear Celia, I already told you: you will never lose your fair for me."

Celia smirks, "Shakespeare again. He always knew how to get the girls into bed."

Jack raises an eyebrow. "A bed, you say? How about we go to my place tonight and check out my bed?"

"Again so soon?" she teases. "You do have a remarkable refractory period, Dr. Spelling."

"Call me Jack," he tells her. "Tonight, in my bed, call me Jack."

She knows what he is really saying and what goes with it. She thinks about the consequences, the future, the possibilities, and decides to take the wild leap.

"Do you have ice, Jack?" she asks, smirking, ready to face the world beyond her office hours.

Fantasy/Paranormal Romance

Valerie Willis
Cedric the Demonic Knight
Romasanta: Father of Werewolves
The Oracle: Keeper of the Gaea's Gate
Artemis: Eye of Gaea
King Incubus: A New Reign

J.M. Paquette
Klauden's Ring
Solyn's Body
Hannah's Heart

4HorsemenPublications.com